Phonics Friends

Gena and the Magic Bear
The Sound of Soft G

The
Child's
World

By Joanne Meier and Cecilia Minden

The Child's World

Published in the United States of America
by The Child's World®
PO Box 326
Chanhassen, MN 55317-0326
800-599-READ
www.childsworld.com

A special thank you to the Schiller family and Samantha's magic touch.

The Child's World®: Mary Berendes, Publishing Director

Editorial Directions, Inc.: E. Russell Primm, Editorial Director and Project Editor; Katie Marsico, Associate Editor; Judith Shiffer, Associate Editor and School Media Specialist; Linda S. Koutris, Photo Researcher and Selector

The Design Lab: Kathleen Petelinsek, Design and Page Production

Photographs ©: Photo setting and photography by Romie and Alice Flanagan/Flanagan Publishing Services

Library of Congress Cataloging-in-Publication Data
Meier, Joanne D.
  Gena and the magic bear : the sound of soft G /
by Joanne Meier and Cecilia Minden.
     p. cm. — (Phonics friends)
  Summary: Simple text featuring the sound of the soft "g" describes how Gena does magic tricks.
  ISBN 1-59296-295-5 (library bound : alk. paper)
[1. English language—Phonetics. 2. Reading.] I. Minden, Cecilia. II.
Title. III. Series.
PZ7.M5148Ge 2004
[E]—dc22   2004003534

Note to parents and educators:

The Child's World® has created Phonics Friends with the goal of exposing children to engaging stories and pictures that assist in phonics development. The books in the series will help children learn the relationships between the letters of written language and the individual sounds of spoken language. This contact helps children learn to use these relationships to read and write words.

The books in this series follow a similar format. An introductory page, to be read by an adult, introduces the child to the phonics feature, or sound, that will be highlighted in the book. Read this page to the child, stressing the phonic feature. Help the student learn how to form the sound with her mouth. The Phonics Friends story and engaging photographs follow the introduction. At the end of the story, word lists categorize the feature words into their phonic element. Additional information on using these lists is on The Child's World® Web site listed at the top of this page.

Each book in this series has been carefully written to meet specific readability requirements. Close attention has been paid to elements such as word count, sentence length, and vocabulary. Readability formulas measure the ease with which the text can be read and understood. Each Phonics Friends book has been analyzed using the Spache readability formula. For more information on this formula, as well as the levels for each of the books in this series please visit The Child's World® Web site.

Reading research suggests that systematic phonics instruction can greatly improve students' word recognition, spelling, and comprehension skills. The Phonics Friends series assists in the teaching of phonics by providing students with important opportunities to apply their knowledge of phonics as they read words, sentences, and text.

The letter *g* makes two sounds.

The hard sound of *g* sounds like *g* as in:

go and *gas.*

The soft sound of *g* sounds like *g* as in:

giraffe and *huge.*

In this book, you will read words that have the soft *g* sound as in:

magic, orange, large, and *giant.*

Gena likes to do magic tricks.

She uses a magic wand.

She likes to imagine things.

Gena has a bear named Gigi.

Gigi is wearing a small,

orange hat.

Gena waves her magic wand.

Gigi is now wearing a large

red hat.

Gena waves her magic

wand again.

Gigi is now wearing orange shoes. They are too large for the bear!

Gena gives her bear a giant hug.

Magic with you is such fun!

Imagine the magic

you could do!

Fun Facts

Did you know that magic is divided into three categories? Close-up magic is magic that is performed with the magician standing close to audience members. This kind of magic may include tricks involving cards or coins. Magicians who do parlor magic usually perform farther away from the audience. Those who do stage magic typically perform on a stage in a theater.

Florida, California, Texas, and Arizona are the states that produce the most oranges. Orange trees were probably originally grown in Southeast Asia. When Christopher Columbus and other European explorers came to the Americas in the late 1400s and early 1500s, they brought orange seeds with them.

Activity

Preparing an All-Orange Lunch

If orange is your favorite color, invite your friends to a special lunch where everything you serve is the color orange. Foods you eat might include cantaloupe, orange Jell-O, yams, apricots, cheddar cheese, macaroni and cheese, toast with orange marmalade, or even actual orange slices! If you are thirsty, pour some orange juice or orange soda.

To Learn More

Books
About Magic
Brown, Jeff, and Steve Björkman (illustrator). *Stanley and the Magic Lamp.* New York: HarperCollins, 1996.

Egielski, Richard. *Three Magic Balls.* New York: Laura Geringer Books/HarperCollins, 2000.

Fox, Mem, and Tricia Tusa (illustrator). *The Magic Hat.* San Diego: Harcourt, 2002.

About Orange
Pinkwater, Daniel Manus. *The Big Orange Splot.* New York: Hastings House, 1977.

Winne, Joanne. *Orange in My World.* New York: Children's Press, 2000.

Web Sites
Visit our home page for lots of links about the Sound of Soft G:

http://www.childsworld.com/links.html

Note to Parents, Teachers, and Librarians: We routinely check our Web links to make sure they're safe, active sites—so encourage your readers to check them out!

Soft G
Feature Words

Proper Names
Gena

Gigi

Feature Word in the Initial Position
giant

Feature Words in the Medial Position
imagine

magic

Feature Words in the Final Position
large

orange

About the Authors

Joanne Meier, PhD, has worked as an elementary school teacher and university professor. She earned her BA in early childhood education from the University of South Carolina, and her MEd and PhD in education from the University of Virginia. She currently works as a literacy consultant for schools and private organizations. Joanne Meier lives with her husband Eric, and spends most of her time chasing her two daughters, Kella and Erin, and her two cats, Sam and Gilly, in Charlottesville, Virginia.

Cecilia Minden, PhD, directs the Language and Literacy Program at the Harvard Graduate School of Education. She is a reading specialist with classroom and administrative experience in grades K–12. She earned her PhD in reading education from the University of Virginia. Cecilia and her husband Dave Cupp enjoy sharing their love of reading with their granddaughter Chelsea.